the PIRATES who don't do anything and ME!

Written by Mike Nawrocki and Karen Poth

Illustrated by Tom Bancroft

BIG IDEA
BOOKS

Zonderkidz

Zonder**kidz**®

The children's group of Zondervan

www.zonderkidz.com

The Pirates Who Don't Do Anything and Me!
ISBN: 0-310-70725-0
Copyright © 2004 by Big Idea Productions, Inc.
Illustrations copyright © 2004 by Big Idea Productions, Inc.

Requests for information should be addressed to:
Zonderkidz, Grand Rapids, Michigan 49530

All Scripture quotations, unless otherwise indicated, are taken from the
HOLY BIBLE, NEW INTERNATIONAL READER'S VERSION ®.
Copyright © 1995, 1996, 1998 by International Bible Society. Used by
permission of Zondervan. All Rights Reserved.

All rights reserved. No part of this publication may be reproduced, stored
in a retrieval system, or transmitted in any form or by any means—
electronic, mechanical, photocopy, recording, or any other—except for brief
quotations in printed reviews, without the prior permission of the publisher.

Zonderkidz is a trademark of Zondervan.

Editor: Cindy Kenney
Art Direction and Design: Karen Poth

Printed in China
04 05 06 07/HK/4 3 2 1

Following a match
on a hot sunny day
a pirate would look
for another to play.

Most pirates don't mind
getting sweaty and hot.
But like most,
these pirates are certainly not.

"I'm pooped," complained Larry.
"One game is enough.
I'd rather be doing some
indoors kind of stuff!"

"Me too!" Lunt agreed, "Where it's climate-controlled.
Let's go take a nap on our cots in the hold."

But just as the pirates
were starting to snore,
there came a soft rap
on the upper deck door.

"Who could that be
disturbing our rest?"
"Are any of us
expecting a guest?"

"Not me," Pa grumped.
Larry buried his head.
"Then it must be the wind,"
Pirate Lunt said.

Knock! Knock! Knock!

The longer the pirates tried to keep napping,
the louder and louder the stranger kept rapping.
'Til finally Pirate Pa just had to say,
"Whoever that is, would you please go away?"

Knock! Knock! Knock!

"Fellas," said Larry, "I think we should check,
and see who is up on the upper-most deck.
Maybe it's someone we *would* like to see,
like a wandering cow selling door-to-door cheese."

Knock! Knock! Knock!

"It could be a scout selling caramel delights,
with coconut frosting in yummy-sized bites."
"Whoever it is, they've ruined our slumber.
They'd better have food!" said Larry Cucumber.

"That knock was so loud
I think it could be
a spaceman who's brought us
some moon crater tea.

I read it all here in my comic book ... see?"

Knock! Knock! Knock!

Those knocks were way too loud to ignore.
The three lazy pirates ran for the door.

They threw it wide open and what did they see?
Just Junior Asparagus. No cookies. No tea.

"Hi Fellas!"
the little one said with a smile.
"I've been up here knocking
for quite a long while!"

They didn't see food,
though each of them tried.
Still Larry said, "Hi Junior!
Come on inside!"

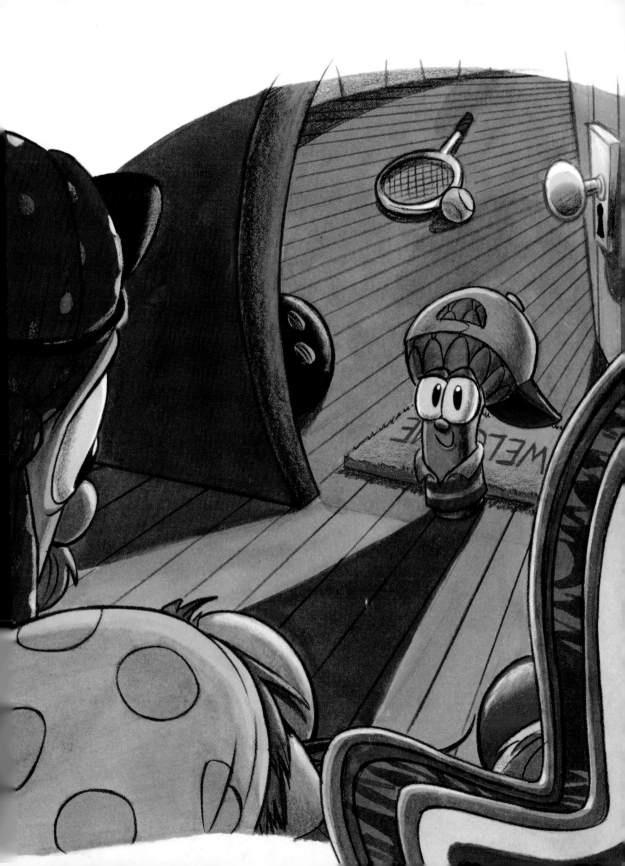

"Now tell us," Lunt said, "just why you would choose
to come without snacks and ruin our snooze?"
"That's easy," he said to the ship's lazy crew.
"I want to do nothing, exactly like you!"

"I like the idea of napping and playing,
so now that I'm here, I think I'll be staying.
Here's what I'm planning—what fun it will be
The Pirates Who Don't Do Anything and ME!"

Junior went on to explain his new plan—
not wanting to go to his school on dry land.
At school there was much that had to be done.
There just wasn't time to have any fun!

"Not like *you* Pirates,
you guys always have fun,
taking naps in the shade,
playing games in the sun.

I want to do nothing.
I think that is cool.
Much better than homework and
going to school!"

"Look Junior," said Larry. "I hear your complaining,
but school is important for pirates in training.

Reading books is required for crewmates on staff,
for adding up nap times, you'll need to know math!"

"Knowing food history helps plan out our snacking.
The Greeks were the first to make pancakes for stacking."

"To be a good pirate,
you must know this stuff.
Just playing and napping
aren't nearly enough."

"And once you're in school,
you might even see
that there are some other things
you'd *rather* be.

As tempting and pleasant
as our lives may seem,
not everyone's meant
for this piratey dream.

Consider our words—
every one of 'em's true!
Then you can ask God
what *he* wants you to do."

Junior thought hard and started believing.
Then he smiled and said, just before leaving,
"I'll make sure that I get a good education,
and visit you guys on summer vacation!"